This book

No Wolves

This is the story of three little pigs,

and houses built of straw, bricks, and twigs.

There's something else.

Can you guess what?

On every page there's a pot to spot!

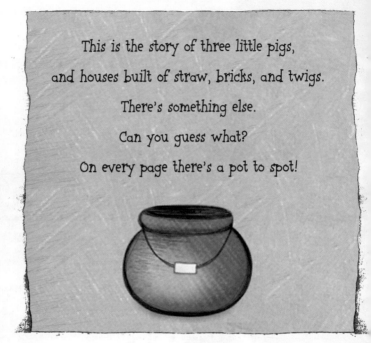

Text copyright © 2007 Nick and Claire Page

This edition copyright © 2011 make believe ideas ltd.

27 Castle Street, Berkhamsted, Herts, HP4 2DW. All rights reserved.

Three Little Pigs

Nick and Claire Page

Illustrations by Katie Saunders

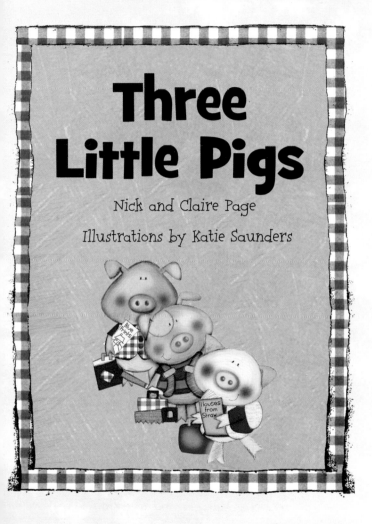

make
believe
ideas

Three little pigs left home one day,
packed their bags and went on their way.
Mother Pig said, "Good-bye, bye, bye!"
But a wolf saw them go and thought,
"Mmm — PORK PIE!"

7

The first little pig met a man selling straw.
"Will it make a good house? I'm not quite sure."
So he paid for the bales and stacked them high,
but the wolf licked his lips, thinking,
"Mmm — STIR FRY!"

9

The second little pig met a man selling wood.
"I think I'll build with this, it looks quite good."
So he worked all day and did not stop,
but the wolf licked his lips, thinking,
"Mmm — PORK CHOP!"

25% off

Edward
Woodwood
Supplies

ward
Wood
plies

11

The third little pig met a man selling bricks.
"These look strong, much better than sticks."
So he built his house, all shiny and new,
but the wolf licked his lips, thinking,
"Mmm — BARBECUE!"

top
sand

12

When the homes were finished
by the piggies three,
they went inside to have some tea.
But the wolf was feeling very hungry too,
and the wolf licked his lips, thinking,
"Mmm — PORK STEW!"

15

Said the wolf to Piggy Straw, "Now let me in!"
"Not by the hair on my chinny chin chin!"
So the wolf huffed and puffed,
and the house went WHAM!
And the wolf licked his lips, shouting,
"Mmm — BOILED HAM!"

17

Piggy Straw ran straight
to the house of Piggy Wood.
And behind him came the wolf,
"Let me in! I'll be good!"

Then he huffed and he puffed,
and the house went SMASH!
And the wolf licked his lips, shouting,
"Mmm — GOULASH!"

Then the two pigs ran
to the house made of bricks.
They were chased by the wolf
(who was not quite as quick).
There he huffed and he puffed,
but the house stayed whole.
So, the wolf climbed the roof, shouting,
"Mmm — CASSEROLE!"

No Salesmen
No Wolves
Please!

Then the three pigs ran
and they fetched a pot.
"Quick, quick," said Piggy Bricks,
"let's make it hot!"
As the hungry wolf jumped
down the chimney tower,
he landed in the pot and screamed,
"Oww — SWEET AND SOUR!"

23

He jumped out quick and ran far away
from the bricks, the wood, and the pile of hay.

And the lesson of this story is —
learn it quick —
don't be a silly sausage —
make your house out of bricks!

Ready to tell

Oh no! Some of the pictures from this story have been mixed up! Can you retell the story and point to each picture in the correct order?

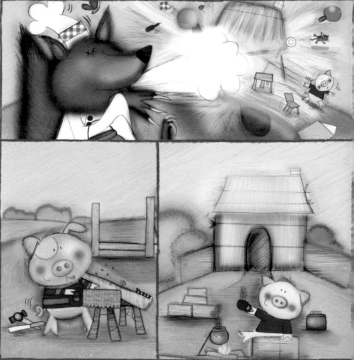

27

Picture dictionary

Encourage your child to read these words from the story and gradually develop his or her basic vocabulary.

bricks

build

chimney

climbed

house

pot

straw

wolf

wood

I • up • look • we • like • and • on • at • for

Key words

Here are some key words used in context. Help
your child to use other words from the border
in simple sentences.

The three little pigs
pack their bags.

The pig builds a
house out **of** wood.

"**I** will blow your house
down!" says Mr Wolf.

Mr Wolf falls into
a pot of hot water.

Mr Wolf runs **away**.

a • he • is • said • go • you • are • this • going • they • away • play • cat • to

day • get • come • in • went • was • of • me • she • see • it • yes • can • am

the • dog • big • my • mom • no • dad • all

Build a house

The three little pigs were good at building houses. Now it's your turn - here's how!

You will need
3 small cardboard boxes • scissors • glue • felt-tip marker • paper • cardboard • straw • twigs • paint • sponge

What to do
1 Cover each box with paper and glue it on.
2 Use the marker to draw a door and windows. Ask a grown-up to help you cut them out.
3 Glue the straw or twigs onto the sides of two of the boxes. For the brick house, cut a small rectangle of sponge and apply paint. Then stamp rows of bricks on the walls.
4 To make the roof, cut a rectangle out of cardboard and fold it down the middle. Glue on your chosen covering. Put glue on the top edges of your box and carefully attach the roof.

Hints and tips
• If you don't have straw, try using packing material, raffia, yellow tissue, or crêpe paper twisted into strips.
• Use popsicle sticks or toothpicks instead of twigs.
• Make a garden with trees made from pinecones and pigs made from corks!